SHADOWS AND LIGHT

SHADOWS

AND LIGHT

Nine Stories by
ANTON CHEKHOV

Selected and Translated by MIRIAM MORTON
Illustrated by Ann Grifalconi

Doubleday & Company, Inc., Garden City, New York

LIBRARY OF CONGRESS CATALOG CARD NUMBER 68-11575
COPYRIGHT © 1968 BY MIRIAM MORTON
PRINTED IN THE UNITED STATES OF AMERICA
FIRST EDITION

Contents

INTRODUCTION

The Author and His Times

ANTON CHEKHOV is universally regarded as a master of the short story. His several hundred stories permanently established this literary form not only in Russian letters but also in the literatures of the world.

But Chekhov's unmatched contribution to the treasury of the world's short stories and his inspiration to authors that came after him, were not his only great achievements. He was also a major playwright and a practicing and crusading physician. And all this Anton Chekhov, a modest, gentle, but determined man, accomplished in a brief lifespan, for his time on earth was cut short by tuberculosis at the age of forty-four.

He was born in 1860 in the small, backward southern town of Taganrog on the Azov Sea. His father

7

was a poor grocer, and the son of a serf. As a boy Chekhov had to help out in the unheated store for many hours daily. In the winter he had to do his schoolwork there, often in near-zero temperatures. The ink in the inkwell would freeze, and his fingers would get numb with the cold. As a result he would sometimes get a failing grade the next day at school and a severe beating for his poor showing from his father.

There were two other helpers around the store—apprentices—whose lot was even more miserable than Antosha's, for these boys would get only crusts to eat, would receive worse beatings, and would be assigned harder tasks to do. The young Chekhov's compassion for the two unfortunates later inspired some of his stories of despairing childhood, among them "Van'ka," offered in this collection.

His father's business failed and the family moved to Moscow, leaving Antosha in Taganrog to finish high school. The boy had to be entirely self-supporting and earned his meager living tutoring reluctant or retarded schoolboys, trudging through the muddy town to the students' homes, in boots full of holes. When he was graduated he joined his family in the capital. There he had to continue earning his living and had to help his impoverished family while attending medical school. Out of dire need for income, Chekhov turned to writing short pieces for newspapers and magazines. The remuneration for these literary efforts was very small, so Chekhov learned to write rapidly and briefly. This was his initial incentive for writing in the short-story medium.

By the time he became a doctor, in 1884, Chekhov was well on the way to becoming an author. A few years later he chose writing as his life's work, though he continued to practice medicine in a limited way, took an active interest in public health, and offered his help unstintingly during epidemics that were frequent and that especially afflicted the poor. (It was in his young adulthood, strained by a heavy load of medical and literary work and the burden of personal poverty, that Chekhov first contracted tuberculosis.)

The stories in this volume were published between 1885 and 1895. Chekhov's career as short-story writer is related to his practice of medicine as well as his latent talents as playwright. Two of the stories included here give the author's observations as a medical man. He knew well how primitively inadequate was the medical aid to the poor and their children (as in "The Fugitive") and the ridiculous superstitions through which the simplest medical phenomenon was often viewed even by the well-to-do (as in "A Horsy Name"). And, although Chekhov wrote most of his short stories before any of his famous plays, he gave them the three-dimensional vividness usually found only in works for the stage. His characters and scenes of action come to life with the playwright's sense of verbal economy and instinct for the dramatic or the comical. "A Day in the Countryside," which Chekhov actually called a *scene* rather than a story (although he wrote it as a short story), "Whose Fault Was It?" and "The Evildoer" are excellent examples of the skill of the dramatist enlivening the short story. Happily, all of the tales offered in this book show an abundance of the same skill.

Chekhov's special gifts as a short-story writer are: authentic observation, well-chosen detail, simple structure, consistency of tone, clarity, and economy of means for sketching in his characters.

However, to understand and enjoy more fully the finely wrought stories in this book, it would be helpful to know about life in czarist Russia during Chekhov's lifetime, for he was a realist and wrote about what he saw and felt. He describes the life about him in the words of one of his short-story characters, the artist in "The House with the Attic" (not in this volume):

> What matters . . . is that peasants are hard at work every minute of the day. They fall ill from overwork, they spend their lives in despairing worry for their sickly, famished children, in terror of illness and death. They're always being treated for some complaint, they wither and age before their time. . . . Then their children grow up and start off on the same old grind. And so it has been for hundreds of years, with millions living worse than cattle, wondering where their next meal is coming from. . . . Situated as they are, and this is what is so horrible, they have no chance to think of their souls or to remember in Whose image and likeness they were created. Famine, cold, blind fear and overwork—these are the avalanches that block all roads to the life of the spirit, the one thing that distinguishes men from beasts and makes life worth living.

In Chekhov's time the peasantry formed the major part of the Russian population, but the urban poor were not much better off. (The story "Oysters" is about disadvantaged city people.)

It must not be concluded from all this that Chekhov's stories are invariably sad or morbid. There is much pathos in them but also plenty of irony, humor, and optimism. In the nine stories offered in this book, we have some bitter ones ("The Fugitive," "Van'ka," and "Oysters"); a few that might be described as bitter-sweet ("Whose Fault Was It?" "A Day in the Country-side," and "The Evildoer"); and some quite humorous stories ("Overdoing It," "A Horsy Name," and "The Pup"). But even his saddest tales have bright touches of irony and humor. All of the stories have substance.

In these selections Chekhov reveals himself as a man of warm compassion for the most defenseless—children, animals, old people, and the extremely poor. In "Whose Fault Was It?" he presents a satire on a self-important teacher who imposes his backward ideas of pedagogy on a helpless kitten. "The Pup" is a touching and funny story about a dog, a wolf, and a crackpot forester who punishes the innocently playful puppy, which is too young and foolish even to fear the wolf. In "The Evil-doer," Chekhov defends an ignorant old peasant who, pathetically and ludicrously uncomprehending of the let-ter of the law, is victimized nonetheless by an officious magistrate who is just as ignorant of the peasant men-tality. The sick child in "The Fugitive" is reduced to a state of panic by the thoughtlessness of an irrespon-sible doctor. The prosperous and boorish city man in "Overdoing It" intimidates the simple, harmless old peasant who has offered him a ride through the wintry forest, which nearly causes the humorous undoing of the gentleman from the city.

Anton Chekhov's stories do not, however, merely tell of life in the Russia of his time as seen by a sensitive and gifted writer. They are timeless. They unforget-tably reveal to the reader the depths and the heights of essential human (and animal) nature. The reader, young or mature, easily recognizes, responds to, and feels for the characters in these stories because they tell of things that still concern, disturb, oppress, inspire, or amuse us today.

Miriam Morton

The Fugitive

It was a long process. First Pashka walked with his mother in the rain across the harvested field and over the forest paths, where yellow leaves clung to his little boots—they walked till sunrise. Then followed two hours of waiting in the dark entry for the clinic to open. It wasn't so cold and raw in the entry as outdoors, but whenever the wind rose outside, a spray of rain would blow in. When the place became filled with people, Pashka was squeezed tight among them, and he leaned his face against someone's sheepskin coat smelling strongly of salted fish and dozed off. Finally the latch clicked, the door was thrown open, and Pashka and his mother entered the waiting room. Here, too, there was

15

a long delay. The patients sat on benches without moving or speaking. Pashka stared at them and was also silent as he was observing much that was strange or funny to him. Only once, when a young man hopped into the room on one leg, Pashka, who also felt like hopping, nudged his mother's elbow, laughed shyly into his sleeve, and spoke:

"Mamma, look—like a sparrow."

"Quiet, little one, be quiet!" his mother whispered.

The clinic attendant finally stuck his head through a small window:

"Line up to register," he bellowed.

Everyone, including the comical hopping fellow, approached the window. The attendant asked each one his name, patronymic, age, place of residence, how long he had been sick, and so forth.

Pashka learned from his mother's answers that his name was not Pashka but Pavel Galaktionov, that he was seven, that he was illiterate, and had been sick since Easter.

The registering finished, everyone had to rise for a moment when the doctor walked across the waiting room, wearing a white apron over which he had tied a towel. Passing the hopping one, the doctor shrugged his shoulders and said in a singsong tenor voice:

"I see—you are a fool! Now, tell me, aren't you a fool? I told you to come back on Monday, and you show up on Friday. As far as I'm concerned, you needn't come at all. But if you insist on being so foolish, you'll lose your leg."

The young man made a very pitiful face, as though he was about to beg for a handout, and said:

"Forgive me—won't you, please!—Ivan Mikolaich."

16

"Never mind the 'Ivan Mikolaich,'" the doctor mimicked. "You were told to come Monday and you should have done so. You're a fool—that's all there is to it."

They began to call in the patients. The doctor sat in his little examining room and called out their names in turn. From time to time piercing cries, children's wailing, or the doctor's angry remarks could be heard:

"Why are you bawling? Am I cutting your throat or something? Sit still!"

Then it was Pashka's turn.

"Pavel Galaktionov!" the doctor shouted.

The mother was confused for an instant, as though she didn't expect this kind of call, and, grabbing Pashka by the hand, led him into the examining room. The doctor sat at his desk tapping a thick book mechanically with a small mallet, without once looking around at them.

"What hurts?" he asked.

"The youngster has a sore on his elbow, dear sir," the mother answered, her face assuming an expression of great grief over Pashka's sore.

"Undress him."

Puffing, Pashka untied the kerchief around his neck, wiped his nose with it, and leisurely began to take off his short sheepskin.

"Woman, you're not here to pay a social call!" the doctor snapped. "Why are you taking your time that way—you're not my only patient!"

Pashka dropped his coat hastily to the floor, and his mother helped him take off his shirt. The doctor looked at him casually and smacked his bare belly.

"That's quite a tummy you've got there, little one,"

he said. And taking a deep breath, he added, "Well, show me your elbow."

Pashka stole a look at the pan with blood rinsings in it and at the doctor's blood-stained apron and began to cry.

"Mye-ye!" the doctor imitated him. "He's old enough to be married off, the spoiled brat, but he still cries. Shame on you!"

Choking back his tears, Pashka looked up at his mother, and there was a plea written in that look: "You won't tell them at home that I cried at the clinic—will you?"

The doctor examined his elbow, squeezed it, sighed, pursed his lips, then squeezed it again.

"You should get a beating, woman, but there's no one to do it!" he said. "Why didn't you bring him here sooner? His arm is ruined! Take a look at it, you fool—it's the joint that's infected!"

"You are the one who knows about such things, dear sir . . . ," the woman sighed.

"'Dear sir . . .' She lets the kid's arm rot and now it's 'dear sir.' What kind of a worker will he make without an arm? Now you'll have to coddle him for the rest of his life. I bet as soon as you get a boil on your nose you run to the hospital, but you let the boy's arm rot for half a year. You're all the same!"

The doctor lit a cigarette. As he was smoking it, he kept scolding the woman and nodding his head to the rhythm of a song he was humming mentally while thinking of something else. Pashka stood near him listening and watching the smoke. When the cigarette burned itself out, the doctor roused himself and continued in a softer tone of voice:

"Now listen, woman—salves and drops will not cure this. You'll have to leave him in the hospital."

"If it's necessary, dear sir, why not leave him?"

"We'll operate. And you, Pashka, you'll stay here," the doctor said slapping him on the back. "Let your mother go home, and you and I, little one, will remain here. It's nice here at my place, my boy, milk and honey flows here! You and I, Pashka, I'll tell you what we'll do— we'll go and catch songbirds and I'll show you a real fox. Then, we'll go visiting together. What do you say? Will you stay? Your mother will come for you tomorrow. What do you say?"

Pashka looked at his mother questioningly.

"Stay, my child!" she said.

"He'll stay, he'll stay!" the doctor cried merrily. "We needn't talk about it anymore. I'll show him a live fox! We'll visit the fair together and buy lollipops. Marya Denisova, take him upstairs."

The doctor, a gay and easygoing type, was seemingly glad to have some company. Pashka felt like accommodating him, especially since he'd never yet been to a fair and would also most definitely want to take a look at a live fox. But how could he possibly manage without his mother? Giving it some thought, he decided to ask the doctor to send his mother along with him to the hospital, but before he had a chance to open his mouth, the woman attendant Marya Denisova led him up the stairway. He walked along and gaped at everything around him. The staircase, the floors and the door frames—all huge, smooth, and bright—were painted a magnificent yellow and had a delicious smell resembling that of Lenten butter. Everywhere there were hanging lamps, runners of carpet, and brass spigots fixed in the walls. But best of all Pashka liked the bed they put him in and the rough gray blanket. He touched the pillows and the blanket, looked around the ward, and decided that the doctor lived not at all badly.

The ward was not large and had only three beds in it. One of them was unoccupied, the second was Pashka's, and on the third sat an old man with sullen eyes, coughing incessantly and spitting into a mug. From Pashka's bed he could see, through the door, part of the adjacent ward and two of its beds: on one slept a very pale emaciated man with a rubber ice-pack on his head; on the other, his arms spread out, sat a peasant with a bandaged head. The bandage made him look like a woman.

The attendant, having settled Pashka in bed, left and soon returned with an armful of clothes.

"These are for you," she said. "Put them on."

Pashka took off his clothes and, not without some pleasure, began to array himself in his new garments. Having put on the shirt, the pants, and the little gray dressing gown, he surveyed himself with approval and thought of how nice it would be to take a walk through his village in this costume. He imagined himself being sent by his mother to the vegetable gardens by the river to gather some cabbage leaves for the piglet; as he set off, the boys and girls gazed with envy at his dressing gown.

The nurse came into the ward carrying two tin bowls, spoons, and two pieces of bread. One bowl she placed before the old man, the other one before Pashka.

"Eat," she said.

Looking into the bowl, Pashka saw rich cabbage soup and in the soup a piece of meat, and again he decided that the doctor lived not at all badly, and that he wasn't such a cross man as he had seemed at first. Pashka took his time with the soup, licking the spoon clean after each mouthful. Then, when there was nothing but the piece of meat in his bowl, he stole a glance at the old man and felt envious that he still had some soup left. With a sigh he started on the meat, trying to make it last long. But no matter how hard he tried, it was no use—soon the meat too was gone. He had only a piece of bread left. Plain bread isn't very tasty, but what could he do! Pashka hesitated for an instant, then ate it up. The nurse appeared with more bowls. This time they contained roast meat and potatoes.

"And where is your bread?" she asked.

Instead of answering her, Pashka puffed out his cheeks and blew out the air.

"Why did you gobble it up?" she said reproachfully. "Now what will you eat your roast meat with?"

She left and came back with another piece of bread. Pashka had never in his life eaten roast meat and, tasting it now, he found it very good. It disappeared quickly and he had a larger piece of bread left than after the soup. The old man hid one of his pieces of bread in the drawer of his small table; Pashka wanted to do the same but reconsidered and ate his up.

After the sumptuous meal he went for a walk to pass the time. In the next ward, in addition to the patients he could see from his bed, there were four other men. Only one of them paid any attention to him. He was a tall, very gaunt peasant with a morose, hairy face; he sat on his bed and regularly, like a pendulum, bobbed his head and swung his arm. For a long time Pashka couldn't tear his eyes away from him. At first the peasant's pen-

dulum-like nods looked curious to Pashka, as if meant
for general amusement, but when he looked closely into
the man's face, he became uneasy, for he saw that this
man was unbearably ill. Going into the third ward, he
saw two peasants with dark-red faces that looked as if
they had been smeared with clay. They sat motionless
on their beds, and with their strange faces, on which
the features could barely be distinguished, they resembled heathen idols.

"Auntie, why are they like that?" Pashka asked the
nurse.

"They have smallpox."

Returning to his own ward, Pashka sat down on his
bed and waited for the doctor to go catch songbirds
with him or take him to the fair. But the doctor did not
come. In the next ward he could see the figure of the
attendant. He was bending over the patient with the
ice-pack on his head and shouting:

"Mikhailo!"

The sleeping Mikhailo did not stir. The attendant
shrugged and left. As he awaited the doctor, Pashka
scrutinized his neighbor, the old man. He kept coughing
and spitting into the mug; his cough was long-drawn-
out and wheezing. Pashka liked one peculiarity about
this old man: when he coughed he drew in air, making
his chest whistle and hum in different tones.

"Grandpa, what whistles inside of you?" Pashka asked.

The old man didn't answer him. Pashka waited awhile,
then asked:

"Grandpa, where is the fox?"

"What fox?"

"The live one."

"In the forest, of course. Where else would she be?"

24

A long time passed, but the doctor did not appear. The nurse brought in tea and scolded Pashka for not having saved his bread. The attendant returned and tried to wake Mikhailo. It turned blue outside the windows and the lights were turned on in the ward. But still no doctor! It was now too late to go to the fair or to catch songbirds. Pashka stretched himself on the bed and began to think. He remembered the doctor's promise of lollipops, his mother's face and voice, the evening shadows in his hut at home, the oven, the grumbling old woman, Egorovna—and he suddenly felt homesick and sad. Then, remembering that his mother would come for him tomorrow, he smiled and closed his eyes.

He was awakened in the middle of the night by a rustling sound. Someone was moving about in the next ward and talking in loud whispers. In the dimness of the night light and the icon lamp, three figures were doing something at Mikhailo's bed.

"Should we carry him out with the bed and all?" one of them was asking.

"No, let's do it this way—the bed will not go through the door. He died too soon, may the Kingdom of Heaven be his!"

One of the men grabbed Mikhailo's shoulders, another his legs, and his arms and the folds of his dressing gown hung limply in the air as they lifted him. The third—it was the peasant who resembled a woman—crossed himself, and shuffling their feet loudly, the three carried Mikhailo out of the ward.

And from the chest of the sleeping old man came the weird whistling and the humming in different tones. Pashka listened, looked at the dark windows, and jumped out of bed, panic-stricken.

"Mommie!" he moaned in a terrified voice.

And, not waiting for her answer, Pashka dashed into the next ward. There the weak rays of the icon lamp and the night light barely penetrated the dark; the patients, upset by Mikhailo's death, were sitting up on their beds; mingled with the shadows, their disheveled figures looked bulkier, taller, and seemed to be growing bigger and bigger; on the last bed, in the corner, where it was even darker, sat the peasant whose head bobbed incessantly, his arm swinging.

Pashka, without seeing the doors, rushed into the ward of the smallpox patients, and from there into the corridor; from the corridor he flew into a large room where long-haired "monsters" with the faces of hags lay on the beds. Running out of the woman's section, he found himself again in the corridor, noticed the banister of the familiar stairway, and ran downstairs. There he recognized the waiting room in which he had been that morning and began to look for the door leading to the outside.

The latch clicked, there was the smell of cold wind, and, stumbling, Pashka ran out into the courtyard. He had but one thought: to keep running! He didn't know the way, but he felt that if he kept running he would somehow find himself at home, with his mother. The sky was overcast but there was a moon behind the clouds. Pashka ran headlong from the steps, circled the barn, and stumbled over some leafless bushes. He hesitated for a moment, then dashed back toward the clinic buildings, ran around them and stopped again, undecided. In the back of the buildings he saw the graves with their white crosses.

"Mommie," he gasped and rushed back.

Running past the buildings he noticed one lighted window.

The bright red spot seemed spooky in the darkness, but Pashka, petrified with fear and not knowing where to seek safety, turned toward it. To the side of the window was a short flight of stairs and a front door with a white shingle hung on it. Pashka ran up the steps and looked into the window, and he at once felt an overwhelming joy. Through the window he saw the jolly and easygoing doctor sitting at the table, reading a book. Laughing with happiness, Pashka stretched his arms out to the familiar figure and was about to call to him, when some unknown force cut off his breath and struck at his legs—he staggered and, losing consciousness, fell down on the steps.

When he came to it was daylight, and a very familiar voice that had yesterday promised him a trip to the fair, songbirds, and a fox was now saying to him:

"Well, you are a fool, Pashka! Tell me, aren't you a fool?! You should get a beating, but there's no one to do it!"

The Evildoer

B<small>EFORE THE</small> investigating magistrate stood an emaciated little peasant in a striped shirt made of ticking and in patched trousers. His hairy face, covered with smallpox scars, and his eyes, scarcely visible under thick overhanging brows, bore an expression of surly coarseness. His head was overgown with a thicket of long, uncombed hair, giving him the air of a cross spider. He was barefoot.

"Denis Grigoryev," the investigating magistrate began, "step up and answer my questions: On the seventh day of the present month of July, the railroad watchman Ivan Semyonov Akinfov, checking the rails on that morning, caught you at the one hundred and forty-first milepost unscrewing the nut of one of the bolts that fasten the rails to the ties. Here is the nut. With said nut he detained you. Is that correct?"

"What d'ye say?"

"Did all that take place as described by Akinfov?"

"Yes, it was so."

"Very well. Tell me, then, why did you unscrew the nut?"

"What d'ye say?"

"Never mind the 'what-d'ye-says' and answer my question: Why did you unscrew the nut?"

"If I hadn't needed it, I'd not have unscrewed it," Denis muttered throatily, with a furtive glance at the ceiling.

"For what purpose did you need it all of a sudden?"

"The nut? . . . We make sinkers out of the nuts."

"And who is 'we'?"

"Us, the common folk—the Klimovo peasants, that is . . ."

"Listen, don't you play the fool with me and talk sense. It won't do you any good to lie to me about sinkers!"

"I've never lied in my life, so why would I start lying now?" Denis grumbled, blinking. "Can it be, Your Honor, that you believe one can fish *without* sinkers? If you cast live bait or worms on a fishhook, would it go down to the bottom without a sinker? . . . And you say *I'm* lying . . ." Denis smirked. "What the devil is the use of live bait if it is going to float on the surface! The perch, the pike, and the eel are always on the bottom, and if the bait floats on the water it will only catch a bullhead and only once in a while at that. Besides, there are no bullheads in our river—this fish likes lots of room . . ."

"Why are you bothering me about bullheads?"

"What d'ye say? Didn't you ask me yourself? . . . Around here even the gentry catch fish that way. Even the smallest urchin wouldn't think of fishing without a sinker. Of course, someone with no sense at all might try it without a sinker—rules aren't made for fools . . ."

"So, you state that you unscrewed this nut in order to use it as a sinker?"

"What else? Not to play knucklebones with!"

"But you could have used a piece of lead, or a bullet, or some kind of nail . . ."

"You don't find lead lying around to be picked up, you have to buy it, and a nail's no good. There's nothing better than a nut. It's heavy and it's got a hole."

"He keeps acting the fool! You might think he was born yesterday or dropped out of the sky! Can't you get it through your thick skull what all this unscrewing can lead to? If not for the watchman, the train might have gone off the rails, people might have been killed! You would have killed these people."

"God forbid, Your Honor! Why would I want to kill people? Am I not a Christian—am I some kind of criminal? Praise be to God, my good sir, I've lived all my life not only without killing but without even thinking of such a thing. Save us and have mercy upon us, Queen of Heaven!—how can you even say such a thing?"

"And, according to you, what causes train wrecks? Unscrew two or three nuts and you'll have a train wreck!"

The peasant smirked and screwed up his eyes at the investigating magistrate, expressing disbelief.

"You don't say! How many years have all of us here in the village been unscrewing those nuts and, the Lord protect us!—there've been no wrecks, no people killed. Now, if I'd carried off a rail or, let's suppose, if I'd put a log in the way—then, maybe, the train might've gone off the track . . . but, pfft! just a nut!"

"Do try to get it through your head that nuts hold the rails fast to the ties!"

"We understand that. . . . You'd think we go around unscrewing all of them—the way you talk. We leave lots of them. We don't do it without using common sense . . . we understand . . ." And Denis yawned and made the sign of the cross over his mouth.

"Last year a train went off the rails here," said the magistrate. "Now it's clear why!"

"Forgive me . . . I didn't quite hear what you said . . ."

"I say, it's clear now why there was a train wreck here last year . . . I now understand the cause."

"That's why you've been given a good education—all of you, our benefactors—to understand. . . . The Lord knows to whom to give understanding. . . . You've figured it out properly, but the watchman—a mere peasant like the rest of us, without a brain in his head—grabs me by the scruff of the neck and pulls me in! Yes, as the saying goes: a peasant has the brain of a peasant. Write down also, Your Honor, that he punched me twice in the teeth and once in the chest."

"When your place was searched they found a second nut. Where and when did you unscrew that one?"

"Are you asking about the nut that was hidden under the little red trunk?"

"I have no idea where you hid it, but it was found! When did you unscrew that one?"

"I didn't unscrew it: Ignashka, one-eyed Semyon's sonny, did it for me. I'm talking now about the one under the little trunk, you know, but the other one, the one in the sled outside, in the yard, that one I unscrewed together with Mitrofan."

"Which Mitrofan?"

"With Mitrofan Petrov. Haven't you heard of him? He makes fishnets—sells them to the gentry. He uses many of these nuts: about ten for each net . . ."

"Now, listen. Article 1081 of the Penal Code stipulates that every deliberate damage done to a railroad endangering the transportation along said railroad, and when the accused knows that said damage would result in a disaster—you understand? . . . *knows!* . . . and you couldn't help knowing what this unscrewing would lead to . . . the accused is punishable by banishment and convict labor."

"Of course, you know best! We are ignorant folk—what do we understand?"

"You understand very well what this is all about! You are lying . . . you are faking!"

"Why should I lie? Ask anyone in the village if you don't believe me. Only bleak is caught without a sinker, and a minnow is hardly a fish at all, and even that you can't catch without a sinker."

"Yes, yes, and what about the bullhead?" prompted the magistrate with a mocking smile.

"We haven't got bullheads in our parts. If we cast our lines without a sinker on the surface, with a butterfly as bait, all we get is mullet, and even that only once in a while."

"That's enough of that! Be quiet!"

There was silence. Denis shifted his weight from one foot to the other, stared at the table covered with a green cloth, and screwed up his eyes as though he was looking not at the cloth but at the sun. The investigating magistrate was writing rapidly.

"Can I go now?" Denis asked after a brief silence.

"No. I must place you in custody and send you to prison."

Denis opened his eyes wide and, raising his heavy eyebrows, looked inquiringly at the magistrate: "What d'ye mean—to prison?! Your Honor, I haven't the time for that; I must go to the fair to collect three rubles from Egor—for lard . . ."

"Be quiet! Don't interrupt!"

"To prison! . . . At least if I'd done something . . . all right . . . I'd go. But to be sent to prison for nothing . . . I live a clean life . . . why send me to prison? I didn't steal anything, and as far as I know I've never started a brawl . . . but if you have doubts about those tax arrears—don't believe a word the village elder says . . . ask the permanent member of the village commons —he's no Christian, that elder! . . ."

"Be quiet!"

"I've been quiet enough," muttered Denis, "but that elder . . . whatever lies he's told about the assessment . . . I'd take an oath . . . there are three of us brothers: Kuz'ma Grigoryev, then Egor Grigoryev, and then there's me, Denis Grigoryev . . ."

"You're interfering! Hey, there, Semyon," cried the magistrate, "take him out!"

38

". . . we're three brothers . . . ," grumbled Denis as two husky soldiers seized him and led him out of the room. "One brother is not another's keeper . . . Kuz'ma doesn't pay, then it's me, Denis, who must answer for him . . . some judges! Too bad he's dead, our late master, the General—may he rest in the Kingdom of Heaven!—or he'd show you judges . . . you must know what you're about before you judge and not do it just like that . . . it's all right even to flog a man . . . but for an evil deed . . . justly . . ."

A Day in
the Countryside

A Scene

IT IS CLOSE to nine in the morning.

In the sky a dark mass, the color of lead, is moving steadily toward the sun. Red zigzags of lightning pierce it here and there. There is a roll of distant thunder. A warm wind brushes over the grass, bends the trees, and raises the dust. Any minute there will be a sprinkle of May rain, and the storm will begin in earnest.

Fyolka, a beggar girl of six, is running through the village looking for the cobbler Terenty. The barefoot, yellow-haired little girl is pale, her eyes are anxious, her lips are trembling.

"Have you seen Terenty?" she asks everyone she meets. No one answers her. They are all busy taking

43

cover in their huts from the approaching storm. At last she meets Silanty Silych, the cobbler's friend and crony. He is staggering in the wind.

"Uncle, where is Terenty?"

"At the vegetable gardens," Silanty answers.

The little beggar girl runs in back of the huts to the vegetable gardens and finds Terenty there. The cobbler, a tall old man with a thin pockmarked face and very long legs, is barefoot and is wearing a torn woman's jacket. He is standing near the vegetable beds looking with his drunken, fish-pale eyes at the dark cloud. He is swaying in the wind on his crane-like legs, like a hanging starling cote.

"Uncle Terenty!" the light-haired little girl says to him, "Uncle, dear!"

Terenty bends down to Fyolka and his sullen, drunken face brightens with a smile, the kind that covers the faces of some people when they regard something tiny, foolish, droll, but deeply loved.

"Ah! Fyolka, God's little one," he says with a soft lisp, "whence has the good Lord sent you?"

"Uncle Terenty," Fyolka says with a sob, pulling at the cobbler's jacket, "brother Danilka is in trouble! Come quick!"

"What kind of trouble? Huh! What thunder! Holy, holy, holy God! . . . What touble is Danilka in?"

"He's stuck his hand into a hollow of a tree—in the Count's grove—and can't get it out! Come, Uncle, get his hand out of there, please!"

"And what made him stick his hand in there? What did he do it for?"

"He wanted to get a cuckoo's egg for me."

"The day has hardly begun and you two are already

44

in trouble!" says Terenty shaking his head and spitting in disapproval. "Well, what am I to do with you! I guess I'll have to go. . . . I guess I must . . . may the wolf gobble both of you up! Troublemakers! Come, let's go, little orphan."

Terenty leaves the vegetable gardens and, lifting his long legs high, sets off down the village street. Taking big strides, and without looking to either side or behind him, he walks on quickly, as though shoved by the wind, or pursued. Fyolka can barely keep up with him.

The pair come to the end of the village and take the dusty road leading to the Count's wood, now looking blue in the distance. It is about a mile and a half away. The clouds have by now covered the sun, and soon there is not a blue patch in the whole sky. It grows dark.

"Holy, holy, holy God!" Fyolka whispers, hurrying after Terenty. The first raindrops, big and heavy, pelt the dusty road with black dots. A large drop falls on Fyolka's cheek and glides like a tear down to her chin.

"There comes the rain," the cobbler mutters, kicking up the dust with his bare bony feet. "For this, thanks be to God, Fyolka girl. The grass and the trees are fed by the rain the way we are by bread. And as for the thunder, don't let it scare you, little orphan. Why should it hurt a tiny thing like you?"

With the downpour the wind calms down. Only the rain makes a noise now as it comes down like fine grapeshot over the young rye and the parched road.

"We'll get soaked, you and I, Fyolushka!" mutters Terenty, "there won't be a dry spot on us. . . . Ha-ha! my girl, it's running down your back now! But don't mind it, little silly, the grass will get dry again, the

earth will dry out, and you and I will get dry too. There is the one sun for all of us."

A fork of lightning two yards long flashes over their heads. There is a loud peal of thunder, and it seems to Fyolka that something huge, heavy, and round is rolling in the sky and tearing it open right over her head.

"Holy, holy, holy God!" Terenty says, crossing himself. "Don't be frightened, little orphan! The thunder means no harm!"

The cobbler's and the child's bare feet become covered with heavy lumps of clay. It is difficult to walk and it is slippery, but Terenty increases his pace. The small, frail beggar girl is breathless and almost ready to drop.

But at last they reach the Count's wood. The wet trees, shaken by a gust of wind, let loose a heavy spray over them. Terenty stumbles over the stumps and slows down.

"Whereabouts is Danilka?" he asks. "Show me."

Fyolka leads him into the grove and, after walking another quarter of a mile, she points to her brother Danilka. A short fellow of eight, with an ocher-red head of hair and a pale, sickly face, stands leaning against a tree and, with his head to one side, is looking up at the sky. In one hand he is holding his worn old cap, and the other is stuck in the hollow of an old linden tree. The boy is scrutinizing the thundering sky and is apparently not paying attention to his predicament. Hearing footsteps and seeing the cobbler, he smiles weakly and says:

"What awful thunder, Terenty! I've never heard such thunder in my whole life!"

"What about your hand? Where is it?"

"In the hole. . . . Pull it out for me, Terenty, please."

A piece of wood had broken off along the edge of the hollow, jamming Danilka's hand. He is able to push it in farther but cannot pull it out. The cobbler removes the broken-off piece and the boy's red and crushed hand is freed.

"What awful thunder!" the boy repeats, rubbing his hand. "What makes the thunder, Terenty?"

"One cloud clashes with another . . . ," the cobbler explains.

The three come out of the wood and walk along the edge toward the darkened road.

The thunder subsides gradually, and its rumbling is now heard from far beyond the village.

"Some ducks flew by here the other day, Terenty," says Danilka, still rubbing his hand. "They're probably nesting in the marshes nearby." Then, turning to his little sister, he says, "Fyolka, would you like me to show you a nightingale's nest? Do you want me to?"

"Don't you touch it, you'll disturb them!" cautions Terenty, wringing the water out of his cap. "The nightingale is a singing bird, and blameless. He's been given such a voice in his throat to praise the Lord with and give cheer to man. It is a sin to hurt them."

"What about the sparrow?"

"The sparrow you can bother. He's a mean bird and spiteful. He's got the thoughts of a swindler in his head and he doesn't like to see man content. When Christ was being crucified, it was the sparrow that brought nails to his tormentors and cried 'Alive! Alive!'"

A light-blue patch appears in the sky.

"Look," says Terenty, stepping aside carefully, "a routed ant heap. They've been flooded, the rascals!"

The three companions bend over the ant heap. The downpour had destroyed their home, and the agitated insects are scurrying about in the mud and fretting around their drowned companions.

"You'll be all right—you won't perish from it!" the cobbler assures them with a smile. "As soon as the sun warms you a bit, you'll come to. But let this be a lesson to you, fools! Next time don't settle on low ground."

They go on.

"And here are some bees!" cries Danilka pointing to a branch of a young oak tree.

Wet and chilled, the bees are huddled together on the branch. There are so many of them that neither bark nor leaves can be seen. Many of them are sitting on top of each other.

"This is a swarm," Terenty informs the children. "It was flying in search of a home, and when the rain came down on it, it settled in the tree. When a swarm is in flight and you want it to settle, all you do is sprinkle it with water. And if you wanted to get those bees now, all you'd do is bend the branch into a sack and shake it—they'd all drop into it."

Little Fyolka suddenly frowns and scratches her neck. Her brother looks at her neck and sees a big welt on it.

"Hee-hee-hee!" the cobbler giggles. "Do you know, Fyolka girl, how you got that? There are Spanish flies on some of the trees in the Count's wood. Water dripped from them and a drop fell on your neck—that's how you got that swelling."

The sun now appears from behind the clouds and sheds its warm light on the wood, the fields, and our three wanderers. The dark, storm-laden cloud has moved far away, taking the storm with it. The air is now warm and fragrant. There is a smell of wild cherry, clover, and lily of the valley.

"That is used to stop a nosebleed," Terenty says pointing to a shaggy flower. "It helps, too."

There is a whistling and a thundering, but not the kind of thundering that the cloud has just carried away with it. A freight train is rushing past the eyes of Terenty, Danilka, and Fyolka. The locomotive, panting and puffing black clouds of smoke, is pulling more than twenty boxcars. It has tremendous power. The cobbler knows that the children would find it interesting to be told how the locomotive, which is not alive and has no horses to help it, can move and drag along such a load. And Terenty undertakes to explain it all to them:

"It's the steam that's doing it all, children. It's the steam that does the work. You see, it moves that thing by the wheels and . . . that's how it works. . . ."

They cross the track and walk down the embankment toward the river. They walk without any destination, at random, and talk all the time. Danilka asks the questions and Terenty gives the answers.

The old cobbler is ready to answer all the boy's questions—nature holds no secret for him. He knows everything. He can name all the wild flowers, all animals, and rocks. He knows which herbs are used to cure what diseases. He has no trouble telling the age of a horse or a cow. Observing the sunset, the moon, or the birds, he can foretell next day's weather. And Terenty is not the only one who is so wise. Silanty Silych, the innkeeper, the vegetable vendor, the shepherd, and the villagers generally know as much as he does. These people have learned not from books but in the fields, in the forest, on the river bank. Their teachers have been the birds themselves as they have sung to them, the sun when it has left a glow of crimson in the sky at setting, the trees, the wild herbs.

Danilka gazes at Terenty and avidly drinks in every word of knowledge. In the spring, before one tires of the warmth and the ever-present green of the fields, when everything is fresh and fragrant, who would not want to hear about golden maybugs, cranes, the gurgling streams, and the corn growing into ear?

The two of them, the cobbler and the orphan, walk in the fields, talk incessantly, and never tire. They could roam the world endlessly. They keep going, and as they talk of the richness of the earth they don't notice the frail little beggar girl trailing after them. She is worn out and moves with a lagging step. There are tears in her eyes. She would be glad to leave these tireless wanderers, but where and to whom can she go? She has no home or people of her own and, whether she likes it or not, she must go on walking and listening to their talk.

Toward noon all three sit down by the river. Danilka takes out of his bag a piece of bread, soaked and soft as mush, and they eat. Terenty says a prayer, kneeling on the sandy bank, then falls asleep. As the cobbler sleeps, the boy looks out at the water, thinking. He has many things to think about. He has just seen the storm, the bees, the ants, the train. Now he can see fishes whisking about, some are two inches long or more, others are no bigger than one's nail. A viper, its head held high, is swimming from one bank to the other.

Only toward evening do the three companions return

to the village. The children go for the night to an abandoned barn where the communal corn used to be kept,
and Terenty, leaving them, goes off to the tavern. The
children lie huddled together on the straw.

The boy is not asleep. He peers into the darkness
and it seems to him that he is seeing all that he has seen
during the day: the storm clouds, the sunshine, the birds,
the fish, long-legged Terenty. The crowding impres-
sions, the exhaustion, and the hunger are too much for
him. He is feverish, as though he were on fire, and tosses
from side to side. He longs to tell someone all that is
haunting him now in the night and agitating his soul,
but there is no one to tell. Fyolka is too young and could
not understand.

"I'll tell Terenty tomorrow," he says to himself.

The children fall asleep thinking of the homeless
Terenty, and in the night he comes to them, makes the
sign of the cross over them, and leaves some bread under
their heads. And no one sees his love. It is seen only by
the moon that floats in the sky and peeps casually
through the holes in the wall of the abandoned barn.

Whose Fault
Was It?

My uncle Pyotr Demyanich—a thin, ill-tempered instructor who looked amazingly like a stale smoked fish with a stick stuck through it—as he was getting ready to go to the high school where he taught Latin, noticed that the binding of his Latin grammar had been nibbled by mice.

"Tell me, Praskovya," he addressed the cook in the kitchen, "how come we have mice in the house? Goodness gracious! Yesterday they chewed up my top hat; today they mutilated my grammar. At this rate they'll start eating my clothes next!"

"What do you expect me to do about it? I didn't invite them in!" answered Praskovya.

"Something's got to be done! Take in a cat or something."

"We have a cat, but of what use is he?" And Praskovya pointed to the corner where a black kitten, thin as a matchstick, lay curled up near the broom.

"Why is he of no use?" asked Pyotr Demyanich.

"He's young and still too stupid. You can see, he's not even two months old."

"H'm . . . then he must be trained. That would be more useful than just letting him lie there. We'd better train him."

Having said this, Pyotr Demyanich gave a weary sigh and left the kitchen. The kitten raised his head, looked lazily after him, and shut his eyes again.

The kitten lay there awake, thinking. But about what? Still unacquainted with real life, and still without stored-up experiences, his contemplations could only be instinctive, and he could picture life to himself only in the images he had inherited, together with his flesh and blood, from his ancestors the tigers. His thoughts were in the nature of daydreams. His cat's imagination pictured something like the Arabian Desert, over which moved shadows in the shape of Praskovya, of the stove, of the broom. In the midst of these shadows there suddenly appeared from time to time a saucer of milk; the saucer sprouted paws and began to move, sometimes even showing an inclination to run; the kitten leaped at it and, possessed by a feeling of bloodthirsting greed, sank its paws into it. When the saucer vanished, a piece of meat appeared, dropped by Praskovya; the meat ran off to the side with a squeak of terror, but the kitten, with a bound, nailed it with his claws.

Everything that the young dreamer saw in his imaginings had to do with leaps, claws, and teeth. The soul of another being is obscure, but how much more so is the soul of a cat! How close to the truth were the visions just described may be seen from what followed: Stirred by his daydreams, the kitten suddenly leaped up, looked with glittering eyes at Praskovya, ruffled up his fur, and, bounding, thrust his claws into the cook's skirt. Obviously, he was born to be a mouse catcher, a worthy descendant of his bloodthirsty ancestors. Fate meant him to be the terror of cellars, storerooms, and cornbins, and, had it not been for education . . . However, we shall not anticipate.

On his way home from the high school, Pyotr Demyanich went into a general store and purchased a mousetrap for fifteen kopecks. During dinner he fixed a small piece of minced meat on the hook and set the trap under the couch, where there were piles of his students' old exercise books, which Praskovya used for household purposes. Exactly at six o'clock that evening, when the esteemed Latinist was sitting at the table correcting his students' notebooks, from under the couch there came a sudden *clop*—such a loud one that my uncle started and dropped his pen. He went at once to the couch and lifted up the mousetrap. A trim little mouse, no larger than a thimble, was sniffing the wire bars of its prison and trembling with fear.

"Aha!" gloated Pyotr Demyanich staring at the mouse with malice, as though he was about to give it a bad grade. "We've cau-aught you, you wr-r-r-etch! I'll show you! I'll teach you to eat my grammar!"

Having looked his fill at the victim, Pyotr Demyanich put the trap on the floor and called:

"Praskovya, the mouse has been caught! Bring the kitten over here!"

"Right away!" Praskovya called back, and in a minute she came, carrying the descendant of tigers.

"Capital!" said Pyotr Demyanich rubbing his hands. "We shall now begin his training. . . . Put him down facing the mousetrap. . . . That's right. . . . Let him sniff it and have a look. . . . That's right. . . ."

The kitten stared with surprise at my uncle, at his easy chair, sniffed the trap in puzzlement, then, frightened, probably by the brightness of the lamplight and the attention centered on him, dashed off in panic and ran toward the door.

"Stop!" my uncle shouted, grabbing the kitten by the tail. "Stop you scoundrel! Are you scared of a mouse, you imbecile! Look! It's a mouse! Why don't you look! Well? . . . Look, I tell you!"

Pyotr Demyanich took the kitten by the scruff of the neck and pushed his face against the mousetrap.

"Look, you carrion! Get hold of him, Praskovya, and keep him there. Hold him at the door of the trap. When I release the mouse, you let him go instantly. Do you understand? . . . Instantly let go! Ready? . . ."

My uncle adopted a conspiratorial air and lifted the door of the trap. The little mouse came out timidly, sniffed the air and flew like an arrow under the couch. The kitten, on being set free, darted under the table and raised his tail in the air.

"It got away! It got away!" cried Pyotr Demyanich, looking fierce. "Where is he, the good-for-nothing? Under the table? You just wait! . . ."

My uncle dragged the kitten from under the table and shook him in the air.

"What a wretch!" he growled, boxing the kitten's ear. "Here, take that! . . . And that! You'd better not miss it again! Wr-r-r-etch!"

Next day the cook again heard the call:

"Praskovya, a mouse has been caught. Bring that cat here!"

After the insults of the day before, the kitten had hidden way under the stove and had not left his refuge all night. When Praskovya pulled him out and, carrying him by the scruff of the neck into her master's study, put him in front of the mousetrap, he trembled all over and meowed pitifully.

"Now, let him get used to it first," Pyotr Demyanich directed her. "Let him look and sniff. Look and learn! Stay there! May the plague take you!" he shouted, seeing that the kitten was backing away from the mousetrap. "I'll thrash you! Hold him by the ear! That's right! . . . Now, put him down in front of the trap. . . ."

My uncle slowly lifted the door of the trap. The mouse whisked past the very nose of the kitten, knocked against Praskovya's hand, and streaked under the cupboard; and the kitten, feeling at liberty, took a desperate bound and darted way under the couch.

"He has let another mouse get away!" raved Pyotr Demyanich. "What kind of a cat is that?! Filthy little beast! Hit him! Hit him right by the mousetrap!"

When the third mouse had been caught, the kitten shook all over at the sight of the mousetrap and its occupant and scratched the cook's hand. After the fourth mouse, my uncle was beside himself, kicked the kitten, and ordered:

"Take the nasty thing out of my sight! Get rid of it—this very day! Throw it out! It's good for nothing!"

A year passed. The thin and frail kitten had become a solid and sensible tomcat. Once he was on his way through the backyard to keep an assignation. He had almost reached his destination when he suddenly heard a rustling sound and caught sight of a mouse running from the water trough toward the stable. My hero's fur stood on end, he arched his back, hissed, and, trembling all over, took cowardly flight.

Alas! Sometimes I, too, find myself in the ridiculous position of the fleeing cat. Like the kitten, I had had the honor of being instructed by my uncle—in my case it was in Latin. Now, whenever I happen to see a work of classical antiquity, instead of feeling eager enthusiasm, I recall *ut consecutivum* (consequently), the irregular verbs, the sallow face of my uncle, the *ablativus absolutus* case. . . . I turn pale, my hair stands on end, and, like the cat, I beat a shameful retreat.

Van'ka

VAN'KA ZHUKOV, a boy of nine who had
been apprenticed to the shoemaker Alyakhin three months
ago, was staying up that Christmas Eve. Waiting until
his master and mistress, together with their workmen,
had gone to midnight service, he took from his master's
cupboard an inkwell and a penholder with a rusty pen-
point, and, spreading out a crumpled piece of paper,
began to write. Before tracing the first word, he looked
around uneasily at the doors and the windows, glanced
at the dark icon, on both sides of which stretched shelves
full of lasts, and heaved a broken sigh. The sheet of
paper lay on a bench and Van'ka knelt in front of it.

"Dear Grandfather, Konstantin Makarich!" he wrote. "I am writing you a letter. I send you Christmas greetings and pray that God Almighty bestow upon you all His blessings. I have neither father nor a mommie—you are the only one left to me in this world."

Van'ka raised his eyes to the dark window in which the light of his candle was reflected and clearly imagined his grandfather, Konstantin Makarich, night watchman for the Zhivarev family. He was a short, slight, uncommonly spry oldster of about sixty-five, with a perpetually smiling face and the bleary eyes of a drunkard. By day he slept in the servants' kitchen or joked with the cook. At night, wrapped in a large sheepskin, he walked the rounds of his master's estate tapping with his little mallet. The dogs, Kashtanka and Eel—the latter given that name because of his long black body—followed him with their heads lowered. That Eel was exceptionally polite and gentle. He would gaze up as lovingly at strangers as he would at people he knew. But underneath his politeness and docility there lurked a most cunning duplicity. He was not trusted. No one knew better than Eel how to sneak up and snap at a person's shins, or how to get into the storage room, or how to steal a hen from a peasant. More than once his hind legs had been nearly pulled off, twice was he about to be hanged, he was beaten severely every week, but he always bounced back.

At this moment Grandfather is, no doubt, standing at the gate, screwing up his eyes at the bright red windows of the village church, stamping his felt boots, and playing the buffoon with the servants. His little mallet is tied to his belt. He is beating his arms for warmth, shrugging his shoulders with the cold, and, with an old man's chuckle, is pinching first the maid then the cook.

"How about a pinch of snuff?" he is saying, offering the women his snuff box.

They are taking a sniff of his snuff and sneezing. Grandfather is indescribably delighted, laughing uproariously, and yelling, "Come on, knock the thing off—it has turned into an icicle!"

They are giving the dogs some snuff, too. Kashtanka sneezes, shakes her head, and, offended, walks away. Eel, too well-mannered to sneeze, only wags his tail.

And the weather must be magnificent—the air still, fresh, and transparent; the night is dark, but the entire village is visible with its snow-covered roofs; the smoke is streaming upward from the chimneys, the trees are covered with silvery frost, and the snowdrifts are beautiful. The whole sky must be seeded with winking stars, and the Milky Way must stand out so clearly, as if it had been scrubbed for the holidays and rinsed in snow.

Van'ka sighed, dipped his pen, and went on with the letter:

Yesterday I got a beating. The master dragged me out into the yard by the hair and hit me with his strap because while I was rocking their baby in the cradle I unexpectedly fell asleep. And last week the mistress told me to clean a herring and I began with the tail, and she grabbed the herring and pushed its head into my face. The workmen make fun of me, send me to the tavern for vodka and make me steal the master's cucumbers for them, and the master hits me for it with whatever he can lay his hands on. And there is nothing to eat. In the morning they give me a piece of bread, for dinner I get some mush and for supper again bread, but as for tea or soup, they gobble it all up themselves. They make me sleep on the porch, and when their baby cries, I don't get to sleep at all but have to rock the cradle. Dear Grandpa, show divine mercy, take me back home to the village, this is more than I can stand. I bow down at your feet and will pray to God for you forever . . . take me away from here or I'll die. . . .

Van'ka's chin trembled, he wiped his eyes with his grimy fist and gave a sob, then continued:

I'll crush your snuff for you, I'll pray for you, and if I do anything bad, wallop me all you want. And if you think that I must have some work, I'll beg the steward for Christ's sake to let me clean his boots, or I'll be a shepherd boy instead of Fed'ka. Dear Grandpa, it is impossible to remain alive here, only death awaits me. I'd run away and return to the village on foot but I have no boots and I'm afraid of freezing. When I grow up I'll repay you and will provide food for you and will not let anyone mistreat you, and when you die I'll pray for the peace of your soul, just as for Mommie's. Moscow is a big city, all the houses belong to gentlefolk and there are many horses, but there are no sheep and the dogs aren't mean. Once I saw a nice store, in the window fishing hooks were for sale, already with the line and for different kinds of fish, very good ones, there was even one hook that could hold a forty-pound catfish. And I've seen shops where they sell guns of all kinds, like the master's guns at home, and I'll bet they are a hundred rubles each. And in the meat stores there are woodcocks, trout, and hares, but the clerks don't tell you where they shoot them.

Dear Grandpa, when they have a Christmas tree at the master's house with treats, get a gilded walnut and keep it for me in the little green trunk. Ask the young lady, Olga Ignatyevna, say it is for Van'ka.

Van'ka gave a tremulous sigh and again stared at the window. He remembered how his grandfather had always gone into the forest to get the Christmas tree for his master's family and had taken Van'ka with him. Those were happy times! Grandfather crackled and the frost crackled and, listening to those two, Van'ka crackled too. Before chopping down the fir tree, Grandfather would smoke his pipe and laugh at the freezing Van'ka. The young fir trees, covered with hoarfrost, stood motionless, waiting to see which of them would be struck down. A hare flew like an arrow over the snowdrifts. Wherever did he come from? The grandfather couldn't refrain from shouting:

"Get'im, get'im! The short-tailed devil!"

Grandfather would drag the chopped-down Christmas tree into the master's house, and there they would set to work decorating it. The young lady of the house, Olga Ignatyevna, Van'ka's favorite, would be in charge. When Van'ka's mother was alive and a servant in the big house, the young lady used to give him candy and, not having much else to do, taught him to read and write, count up to a hundred, and even to dance the

quadrille. When his mother died, Van'ka had been moved to the servants' kitchen to be with his grandfather, and from the kitchen to Moscow, to the shoemaker Alyakhin.

Van'ka continued with the letter:

Come and get me, dear Grandpa, for Christ's sake, I beg you, take me away from here. Have pity on me, a miserable orphan. Here everyone hits me, and I'm awfully hungry, and I'm so homesick I can't even tell you how, and I keep crying. The other day the master struck me so hard on the head that I fell down and could hardly get up again. Wretched is my life, worse than any dog's. I send my greetings to Alyona, to one-eyed Egorka, and to the coachman, and don't forget, don't give away my harmonica to anyone. I remain your grandson, Ivan Zhukov. Dear Grandfather, come for me.

Van'ka folded the letter and put it into an envelope he had bought the day before for a kopeck. After thinking for a moment, he dipped his pen and wrote the address:

To Grandfather in the village

Then he scratched the back of his head, thought a little and added: "Konstantin Makarich." Glad that he had been able to write without interference, he put on his cap and, without putting on his little winter jacket, ran out into the street as he was, in his shirt.

The clerks at the butcher shop, whom he had consulted the day before, told him that letters were put in mailboxes and from there were carried to all parts of the world in mail carts with drunken drivers and ringing bells. Van'ka now ran to the nearest mailbox and pushed his precious letter through the slit.

An hour later, lulled by sweet hopes, he was sound asleep. He dreamed of the stove. On it sat his grandfather dangling his bare legs and reading the letter to the cooks.

Eel stood by the stove wagging his tail.

The Pup

A FAMISHED SHE-WOLF got up to go hunting. Her babies, all three of them, were fast asleep, huddled in a heap in each other's warmth. She licked them for a while, then went off.

It was March and the beginning of spring, but at night the trees still crackled with the cold, as in December, and no sooner did one put out his tongue than the cold would nip it hard. The mother wolf was in poor health and fearful. She started at the slightest noise and kept worrying that someone might hurt her young ones while she was away from them. The scent of men and horses, the stumps of trees, the woodpiles, and the dark road strewn with dung, all frightened her.

She imagined people standing in the darkness behind the trees and dogs howling somewhere beyond the forest.

She was no longer young, and her sense of smell had become less sharp, so that it happened that she mistook a fox's track for that of a dog, and sometimes, deceived by her waning sense of smell, she lost her way— a thing that never happened in her youth. Because of feeble health she no longer hunted calves or large sheep and had for some time avoided horses with colts, but nourished herself only on carrion. She now tasted fresh meat only in the spring, when, chancing upon a rabbit, she would steal her young, or when she sneaked into a peasant's cattle-shed where there were lambs.

About two miles from her lair, on the post road, stood a winter lodge. Here lived watchman Ignat, an old man of about seventy, who was always coughing and talking to himself. Usually he slept at night, and during the day he wandered about the forest with his single-barreled gun, whistling to attract the rabbits. In the past he must have worked on a railroad as some sort of trainman, for every time before halting, he would call out to himself: "Stop the engine!" and before going on again he would yell out: "Let it go! Full speed!" He always had with him a huge black female dog of indefinite breed, called Arapka. When she ran ahead of him he would shout to her: "Back up! In reverse!" At times Ignat staggered and fell (the wolf would then think the wind blew him over), shouting: "Off the rails!"

The she-wolf remembered how in the summer and fall a ram and two ewes had pastured near the winter hut, and when she ran past the cattle-shed not so long ago she thought she heard the bleating of lambs inside. And now, approaching the hut, she thought that, judging by the season (it being already March), there certainly would be lambs in the shed. She was tormented by hunger and imagined, as she approached the place, with what relish she would eat a baby lamb, the thought of it making her teeth snap, and her eyes gleamed in the darkness like two coals.

Ignat's hut, barn, shed, and well were surrounded by snowdrifts. All was still. Arapka was probably asleep under the shed.

The mother wolf clambered over the snowdrift and onto the roof of the shed. She began to dig away at the thatch with her paws and muzzle. The straw was rotten and loose, and the wolf almost fell through as the warm vapor and the smell of manure and sheep that came from below overwhelmed her. A baby lamb, feeling the sudden cold, bleated softly. Jumping through the hole in the roof, the wolf fell on her forepaws and chest right against something warm—it must have been the ram. And at the same moment something in the shed began to whine, bark, and yelp in a shrill little voice, while the sheep pressed against the wall. The she-wolf, frightened, grabbed the nearest thing between her teeth and darted away.

She ran as fast as she could, as Arapka, who by now had scented the wolf, let out a furious howl, the agitated chickens chattered inside the hut, and Ignat, coming out on the front steps, shouted:

"Full speed! Blow the whistle!"

And he whistled like a steam engine and let out a "hoo-hoo-hoo-hoo!" And these sounds echoed back from the forest.

When, little by little, this cacophony finally ceased, the wolf calmed down a bit and began to notice that the prey she held in her teeth and dragged along the snow was heavier and seemed harder than young lambs usually were at that time of year, and that the animal had a different smell and emitted strange sounds. The wolf stopped and dropped her burden on the snow to rest and then begin to eat. Suddenly she recoiled in disgust. It wasn't a lamb at all; it was a puppy—black, with a big head and long legs, of a large breed, with a white patch on its forehead, like Arapka's. Judging by his ways, he was a common, ill-mannered yard dog.

The puppy licked his rumpled, wounded back and, as though nothing was wrong, wagged his tail and barked at the wolf. The wolf growled like a dog and ran away from the pup. He followed her. She looked back and snapped her teeth. The pup stopped, puzzled, and, deciding that the wolf was probably playing with him, turned his head in the direction of the hut and let out a gleeful, loud bark, as though inviting his mother, Arapka, to come and join them in the game.

It was beginning to get light, and as the wolf was approaching her lair through the thick aspen forest, one could already see distinctly each young aspen tree; and the woodcocks were waking, the handsome male birds fluttering into the air, disturbed by the frolicsome and barking pup.

"Why is he following me?" thought the wolf with annoyance. "He probably wants me to eat him."

She lived with her cubs in a shallow pit formed three years before when a tall old pine tree had been torn up by the roots during a violent storm. The pit was now lined with dead leaves and moss, and here also were strewn about the bones and horns of bullocks, with which the little wolves played. They were awake now and all three of them, looking very much alike, stood in a row on the edge of the hole, looking at their returning mother and wagging their tails. Seeing them, the puppy stood still at a distance, stared at them for a long time, and noticing that they were staring back at him attentively, he began barking at them angrily, as at strangers.

It was daylight by now, the sun had risen, and the snow gleamed everywhere, but the pup still stood at a distance. The baby wolves were suckling, pressing their paws against the mother's belly, as she gnawed at the bone of a horse, fleshless and white. She was desperately hungry, her head ached from the noise of the puppy's barking, and she felt like throwing herself at the uninvited guest and tearing him to pieces.

At last the pup got tired and hoarse. Seeing that they were not afraid of him and that they weren't even paying any attention to him now, he began to approach the cubs hesitatingly—by turns cowering and taking a few leaps toward them. Now, in full daylight, it was easier to take a good look at him. His white forehead was large and there was a protuberance on it such as very stupid dogs commonly have. His eyes were small, blue, dull, and the expression on his face was extremely foolish. Approaching the cubs, he stretched out his wide paws, rested his head on them, and began to whine.

The cubs didn't understand what was happening, but they wagged their tails. Then the pup smacked one of them on its large head with his paw. The cub smacked him back. The pup jumped sideways, looked at him askance, wagging his tail all the time, then dashed off, and ran around in a circle several times over the frozen snow. The cubs chased after him. He turned over on his back, kicking his legs in the air, and all three of the cubs fell upon the pup, squealing with delight and biting him, not hard, not to hurt, but in play. The crows sat on a tall pine tree and looked down from above upon the skirmish, very upset about it. The young animals grew noisy and merry. The sun gave forth a spring warmth, and the woodcocks, flitting through the pine tree that had been blown down by the storm, looked emerald in the sunshine.

Normally mother wolves train their young to hunt by giving them prey to play with, and now, seeing how the cubs were pursuing the puppy over the snow and wrestling with him, she thought:

"Let them learn."

After having had their fill of play, the cubs went back into the pit and lay down to sleep. The puppy howled for a while from hunger, then, following their example, stretched out in the sun for a nap. And when they woke up, they resumed their play.

All day long and in the evening the mother wolf thought about how the night before the baby lamb bleated in the shed and how it smelled there of sheep's milk, and she kept snapping her teeth with the craving for food as she kept gnawing on an old bone, making believe it was the lamb.

The little wolves suckled their mother, and the puppy, who was very hungry by now, ran around sniffing at the snow.

"I'll eat him," the wolf decided.

She went up to the pup and he licked her face and yapped at her, thinking that she wanted to play with him. In the past she had eaten dogs, but the puppy had a strong doggy scent and, because of her feeble health, the wolf couldn't stand it now. She felt disgusted and walked away.

It became colder toward night. The puppy got homesick and left.

When the baby wolves were fast asleep, their mother went hunting again. Again, as in the previous night, she worried about the slightest noise and was alarmed by the stumps, the logs, the dark solitary juniper bushes looking like human beings from a distance. She ran along the side of the road over the frozen snow. Suddenly, far ahead on the road, something dark came into view. The wolf strained her eyes and ears—there really was something moving there in the distance and she could even hear the regular thud of the footsteps. Could it be a badger? She kept closer to the side of the road and hardly breathed as she cautiously overtook the moving creature. She looked at it. It was the pup with the white patch on his forehead, slowly making his way to the winter hut.

"If only he doesn't spoil my chances again," the wolf thought and ran quickly on ahead.

The hut was now quite near. Again she clambered up the snowdrift and onto the roof of the cattle-shed. The hole she had made the night before had been covered over with cornstalks and two new rafters stretched across the roof. The wolf began to work fast with her legs and muzzle, looking around to see whether the puppy was coming, and barely did she begin to feel the warm air and the smell of manure from below, when she heard a burst of happy barking behind her. The puppy had arrived. He leaped up to the roof then went through the new hole, and, glad to be home, in the warmth, and recognizing his sheep, he barked even louder. Arapka woke up under the shed, smelled the wolf and howled. The hens began to chatter. And by the time Ignat the watchman appeared on the front steps with his single-barreled shotgun, the terrified wolf was already far way from the hut.

"F-ew-ew-t!" whistled Ignat. "F-ew-ew-t! Full steam ahead!"

He pulled the trigger. The gun misfired. He pulled it again, and again it misfired. He tried a third time, and a tremendous flame shot out of the barrel and there was a deafening blast. The recoil jarred his shoulder and, carrying the gun in one hand and an ax in the other, Ignat went to see what the noise was about.

He soon returned to the hut.

"What was it?" a pilgrim, who was spending the night there and had been awakened by the disturbance, asked in a husky voice.

"Oh, nothing," Ignat answered. "Nothing important. Our pup has taken to sleeping with the sheep, to keep warm. Only, he is too stupid to use the shed door and always wriggles in and out of the shed through the roof. The other night he dug a hole in the roof and went on a spree, the rascal, and now he has come back and torn up the roof again."

"Stupid dog!"

"Yes, there is a screw loose in his head. I can't abide fools!" sighed Ignat climbing onto the stove. "Come on, man of God, let's go back to sleep—it's too early to get up—full speed ahead!"

In the morning he called the pup, pulled his ears hard and, whacking him with a stick, kept repeating:

"Use the door! Use the door! Use the door!"

Overdoing It

THE LAND SURVEYOR Gleb Smirnov got off the train at Gnilushka. The station was some twenty miles from the estate he came to survey, and he had to cover that distance in a horse-drawn vehicle of some sort. (When the driver wasn't drunk and the horses weren't nags, the distance was less than twenty miles; but when the driver was tipsy and the horses played out, it seemed more like thirty.)

"Tell me, please, where could I find post horses and a carriage around here?" the surveyor said to the station guard.

"What kind? . . . Post horses? . . . Here for fifty

miles around you couldn't even find a sled dog, let alone post horses. . . . Where are you bound for?"

"For Devkino—the estate of General Khokhotov."

"Well," the guard yawned, "try on the other side of the station. You may find some peasants over there who haul passengers."

The land surveyor made his way across from the station. After looking for some time, then after prolonged negotiations and hesitations, he engaged a husky peasant—glum, pockmarked, and dressed in a tattered gray coarse wool coat and bast-bark shoes.

"What kind of a wagon do you have here!" grumbled the surveyor as he climbed into the wagon. "You can't tell the front from the rear."

"What is there to tell? Near the horse's tail it's the front, and where your lordship is now sitting is the rear."

The horse was young but emaciated, with splayed hoofs and nicked ears. When the driver, raising himself, struck her with his hemp whip, she merely shook her head. When he cursed and struck her a second time, the wagon creaked and shook as if with a bad chill. After the third stroke, the wagon lurched and swayed from side to side, and after the fourth, it moved.

"Is this how we'll proceed all the way?" the surveyor asked, feeling a violent jolting and amazed at the ability of Russian drivers to combine a snail's pace with a jolting that turned one's insides upside down.

"We-e-'ll get there . . . ," the driver assured him. "The mare is a young one, and spirited. Just let her get started at her own pace, then there'll be no stopping her. . . . Giddy-up, you accursed one!"

It was dusk when the wagon drew away from the

station. To the right of the surveyor stretched the dark, frozen plain—broad and endless. Try to cross it and you'll come to the end of the world. On the horizon, where the plain merged with the sky and disappeared, the autumn sun was lazily sinking in the mist. To the left of the road, in the darkening space, loomed oddly shaped mounds, and it was hard to tell whether they were last year's haystacks or the huts of a village. What there was ahead of them the surveyor could not tell because his field of vision was completely obstructed by the massive back of the driver. It was still, cold, frosty.

"What a God-forsaken place this is!" thought the surveyor as he tried to cover his ears with the collar of his greatcoat. Not a man or beast in sight! Who knows what could happen in a place like this—they can attack you and rob you and no one will be the wiser for it. And this driver—he's not very reassuring. . . . Some husky back he's got! And he has the mug of a beast . . . yes, it's all very frightening."

"Tell me, my dear man," the surveyor asked, "what is your name?"

"Mine? Klim."

"Well, tell me, Klim, is it safe around here? No ruffians?"

"No, thank God! What kind of ruffians could there be here?"

"That's good that there are none. But, just the same, to play it safe, I brought along three revolvers," the surveyor lied. "And with a gun, as you know, it's bad business to joke. I can handle ten cutthroats with them!"

95

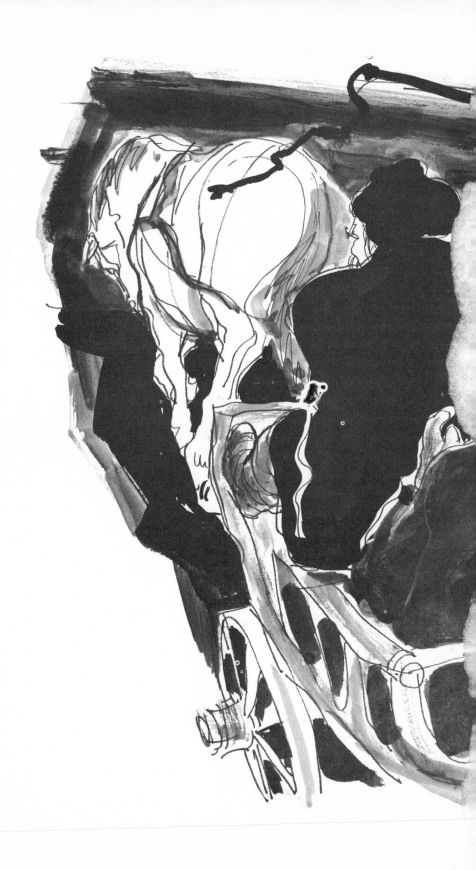

It grew dark. The wagon suddenly creaked, squeaked, shook, and, as though against its will, turned left.

"Where is he taking me?!" the surveyor thought. "He's driving straight ahead and suddenly he turns left. What is he up to? He'll take me, the wretch, into some thicket and . . . and. . . . One hears of such things happening!"

"Listen here," he called to the driver. "You say there's no danger around here? That's too bad! I like to fight off cutthroats. In appearance I'm thin, sickly looking, but I have the strength of a bull! Once three highwaymen threw themselves upon me. And what do you think happened? One of them I socked so hard that he gave up his soul to the Lord, and the other two were sentenced to Siberia to do hard labor because of me. And where I get all this power, I really couldn't tell you. I can grab a husky fellow—like you—and knock him down flat!"

Klim looked around at the surveyor, made a wry face, and struck the horse with the whip.

"Yes, brother . . . ," continued the surveyor, "may God help those who tangle with me! Not only will the cutthroat remain without arms and without legs, but he will be dragged off to court as well. I'm acquainted with every district judge and police inspector. I'm a civil servant, you know, and an important one at that. I'm in transit now, but the officials know about this journey . . . they're watching that no one does me any harm. Everywhere along the way, behind the bushes over there, are deputized village police inspectors and policemen. "St-o-o-o-p!" the surveyor suddenly screamed. "Where did you drive into now? Where are you taking me?"

"Can't you see? Into the forest."

"That's right—it's a forest . . . ," thought the surveyor. "And I got scared! However, I must not show my fear. He's noticed already that I'm scared. Why has he been looking around at me so much? He's probably planning something. . . . Before he crawled along, and now look at him speed!"

"Listen, Klim, why are you hurrying your horse this way?"

"I'm not hurrying her. She is speeding of her own free will. I suppose she herself isn't pleased to have legs that make her go that fast."

"You're lying! I can see that you're lying! But I'd advise you not to rush that way. Rein in your horse! Do you hear me? Rein it in!"

"Why?"

"Because . . . because four pals of mine are joining me here . . . from the station. We must let them catch up with us. They promised to catch up with me in this forest. . . . It will be merrier to travel with them. . . . They are tough fellows, thick-set . . . each one is armed with a pistol. . . . Why do you keep looking around and fidgeting as if you were on pins and needles? Why? There is nothing to look at . . . there is nothing especially interesting about me . . . just my guns, perhaps . . . if you want me to, I'll get them out and show them to you . . . if you want . . ."

The surveyor dug into his pockets for the imaginary guns. And then something unexpected, something that he did not foresee in all his cowardice, happened. Klim suddenly rolled off the wagon and almost on all fours rushed into a thicket.

"Help!" he wailed. "Help! Take the horse and the wagon, and be damned, but don't kill me! Help!"

The surveyor heard the departing steps of the driver, the crackling of the underbrush—then complete silence. Not expecting such a verbal attack, the surveyor first of all stopped the horse, then sat back more comfortably in the wagon and gave himself over to thought.

"He ran off . . . got scared, the fool! What'll I do now? I can't go on by myself because I don't know the way, and also, I might be suspected of stealing his horse. . . . What had I better do?"

"Klim! Klim!"

"Klim!" answered the echo.

The thought that he might have to spend the night sitting there in the cold dark forest, hearing only the wolves, their echo, and the neighing of the emaciated mare, sent shivers up and down the surveyor's spine, as though it were being scraped with a cold file.

"Klimushka!" he cried. "My dear man! Where are you, Klimushka?"

The surveyor called for about two hours, and only after he became hoarse and resigned himself to spending the night in the forest, did a soft wind carry to him the sound of someone's groaning.

"Klim! Is that you, my dear man? Let's go on!"

"You'll ki-i-i-ill me!"

"I was just joking, my man! May God punish me if I wasn't joking! I have no guns! I lied because I was scared! Do me a favor, let's go on! I'm freezing to death!"

Klim, having perhaps decided that a real cutthroat would have long since got away with his horse and wagon, emerged from the thicket and hesitantly approached his passenger.

"What was there to get scared about, you fool? I . . . I was just kidding, and got scared. . . . Get in!"

"I'll have nothing more to do with you, master," Klim muttered, climbing up into the wagon. "Had I known, I wouldn't have taken you on, not for a hundred rubles. You nearly made me die of fright."

Klim struck the horse with his whip. The wagon trembled. Klim struck again, and the wagon lurched. After the fourth time, when the wagon moved, the surveyor covered his ears with his collar, and meditated. The road and Klim no longer seemed to him threatening.

Oysters

I DON'T NEED to strain my memory much to recall in every detail that rainy day when, at dusk, I stood with my father on one of the crowded Moscow streets and sensed that I was being stricken by a strange illness. I felt no pain, but my legs were giving under me, the words stuck in my throat, and I didn't have the strength to keep my head from falling to one side. It seemed as though any moment I'd fall down and lose consciousness.

Had I been taken to the hospital, the doctors would have had to write on the diagnosis chart over my bed: "*Fames* [starvation]," a disease not listed in manuals of medicine.

Near me, on the sidewalk, stood my father wearing a threadbare summer overcoat and a knitted quilted cap from which a bit of white wadding was sticking out. He had on large heavy galoshes. Fearing, vain man, that people would notice that he was wearing the galoshes over his bare feet, he had drawn the tops of a pair of discarded boots over the calves of his legs.

This poor, odd-looking man whom I loved the more warmly the shabbier and dirtier his fancy summer coat became, had come to Moscow five months before in search of a position as copying clerk. He had trudged daily through the city during those five months asking everywhere for work, and it was only on that day that he finally gave in and went into the streets to beg.

Across the street from where we were standing was a three-story building on which hung a blue sign with the word *Traktir* [Tavern] on it. My head was swaying weakly backward and to the side, and I couldn't help looking up to the lighted windows of the tavern. I saw human figures moving inside past the windows. I could also see the side of a large mechanical music box, two oil paintings, and the hanging lamps. Then my eyes caught a white spot on one of the windows. The spot was motionless and stood out sharply—white and rectangular—from the dark-brown background of the rest of the window. I kept staring at it and gradually realized that it was a white placard. Something was written on it, but I couldn't make out what it was.

For the next half hour or so I didn't tear my eyes from this placard. Its whiteness held my vision and seemed to hypnotize my brain. I kept trying to read what it said, but my efforts brought no results.

At last the strange malady took full control over me.

The noise of the traffic began to sound to me like thunder. In the stench of the street I discerned a thousand smells, my eyes saw blinding lightning in the tavern lamps and the street lights. All my five senses were extremely keen and abnormally sensitive. I now began to see clearly what I couldn't decipher before:

"*Ustritsy* [Oysters]" I made out on the window placard.

A strange word! I had lived on this earth exactly eight years and three months but had never once heard this word. What could it mean? Was it perhaps the name of the proprietor of the tavern? But signs with names were hung over doors not on windows.

"Papa, what does 'oysters' mean?" I asked in a low, hoarse voice, trying hard to turn my face toward my father.

He did not hear me. He was busy scrutinizing the moving crowd and following each pedestrian with his eyes. I could see that he wanted to say something to the passers-by but the mortifying word hung like a heavy weight on his trembling lips and refused to be uttered. He even took a few steps after a pedestrian and touched his sleeve, but when the man turned around my father cringed and said "Forgive me" self-consciously, and drew back.

"Papa, what does 'oysters' mean?" I repeated.

"It's a kind of animal . . . it lives in the sea . . ."

Instantly a strange sea creature materialized in my imagination. It must be a cross between a fish and a crab, I thought. And as it was from the sea, they no doubt made out of it a very tasty hot fish soup with fragrant pepper and laurel leaves, or broth with vinegar and fish giblets, or served it cold with crab sauce and horseradish. I vividly pictured to myself how this animal was brought from the marketplace, quickly cleaned, and quickly put in a pot to cook . . . quickly, quickly, for everyone was hungry . . . terribly hungry! From the kitchen came the smell of baked fish and crab soup.

I felt this smell tickling my palate, my nostrils, and gradually penetrating through my whole body. The tavern, my father, the white placard, my sleeves—everything smelled of it strongly, so strongly that I began to chew. I was chewing and swallowing as though a piece of this sea animal was actually in my mouth.

My legs gave way from the delicious pleasure I felt and, to keep myself from falling, I grabbed my father's arm and leaned against his wet summer coat. My father was shivering and drawing himself together. He was cold.

"Papa, is it all right to eat oysters during Lent, or are they forbidden?" I asked.

"They're eaten alive," my father answered. "They're in shells, like turtles, but in two halves."

The savory smell at once stopped tickling my body and the illusion vanished. Now I understood everything clearly!

"How disgusting!" I muttered. "How disgusting!" So that's what oysters were like! I now imagined to myself this creature as resembling a frog. The frog was sitting inside its shell and staring from it with its large eyes as he worked his hideous jaws. I pictured it being brought from the marketplace inside its shell, with its claws, beady eyes, and slimy skin. The children hid from it, while the cook, frowning with disgust, picked it up by a claw, put it on a plate, and carried it to the dining room. The grown-ups took it and ate it—they ate it alive, eyes, teeth, claws, and all, as the creature squealed and tried to bite their lips.

I felt aversion, but why did my teeth begin to chew? The creature was nasty, frightening, but I kept eating—eating greedily, avoiding feeling its taste and smell. As I finished off one, I already saw the glittering eyes of the second, the third. I ate these up too. Then I ate the napkin, the plate, my father's galoshes, the white placard. I gobbled up everything in sight, for I was convinced that eating would cure my illness. The oysters' eyes scared me and they were revolting, and I shook at the thought of them, but I wanted food! Food!

"Oysters! Give me oysters!" the cry broke from me and I reached out my hands for some.

"Help us, gentlemen!" I heard at that moment my father's hollow and strained voice. "I'm ashamed to beg but . . . my God! . . . I can't stand it any more!"

"Give me oysters!" I kept on, pulling at my father's coat.

"Do you mean to say you eat oysters?—a little fellow like you!" I heard someone near me say with a laugh.

Two gentlemen in top hats were standing before us, looking into my face and guffawing.

"Do you really eat oysters, little urchin? That's interesting! Come, tell us how you eat them."

I remember someone's strong arm pulling me toward the lighted tavern. Within a minute I was inside and a crowd was staring at me with curiosity and amusement. I was sitting at a table now and eating something slippery and salty with a smell of dampness and moldiness. I ate avidly, without chewing, without looking to see what it was that I was eating. I felt that if

I opened my eyes, I would be staring straight into those beady eyes, claws, and pointed teeth.

All of a sudden I began to chew something hard. There was a sound of crunching.

"Ha-ha-ha! he's eating the shell!" the crowd laughed. "Little fool, you don't eat that, you little fool!"

Afterward I remember having an awful thirst. I lay in bed unable to sleep from the heartburn and the strange taste in my parched mouth. My father was pacing the room, gesticulating with his hands.

"I think I've caught a cold," he was mumbling. "I have a queer feeling in my head . . . as if someone is sitting inside . . . but maybe it's because I've had nothing to eat today. . . . I'm a stupid sort of person,, I suppose . . . I saw those gentlemen pay ten rubles for the oysters—why didn't I go up to them and ask for a few . . . just as a loan? . . . They'd probably have given me something . . ."

I fell asleep toward morning and dreamed of a frog with claws sitting in a shell and blinking its eyes. I was awakened by thirst and looked for my father. He was still pacing the room and gesticulating.

A Horsy Name

THE RETIRED major-general Buldeyev had developed a bad toothache. He rinsed his mouth with vodka, then with brandy, applied tobacco ashes, opium, turpentine, and kerosene to the aching tooth, painted his cheek with iodine, put cotton soaked in alcohol into his ears—but none of these remedies helped, and some of them made him sick to his stomach.

The doctor came. He poked at the tooth, prescribed quinine, but neither did this relieve the pain. To the suggestion that he have the tooth extracted, the general said a categorical no. The entire household—his wife, children, domestics, even the kitchen boy Pet'ka— each offered his favorite remedy. Among others, the general's steward, Ivan Evseich, came to him and advised him to have the tooth cured by exorcism.

"Here, in our district, Your Excellency," said he, "some ten years ago lived a tax assessor, Yakov Vasilich. His incantations were first rate! He would turn toward a window, whisper something, spit—and the pain would disappear as though removed by hand. He certainly possessed that kind of power!"

"And where can he be reached now?"

"After he was dismissed as tax assessor, he went to live at his mother-in-law's, in Saratov. And now he's making a living entirely out of teeth. When anyone has a toothache, he goes to Yakov Vasilich and is cured. Local patients he treats in his home; those who live out of town he cures by telegraph. Why not send him a wire, Your Excellency?—telling him thus and so: 'I, servant of the Lord, Aleksei, have a toothache that I beg you to treat.' The fee you can send him by mail."

"Stuff and nonsense! Quackery!"

"Why not try it, Your Excellency! He's fond of his liquor and curses like a trooper, but one can't deny that he's a real miracle worker!"

"Do send for his help, Alesha!" the general's wife pleaded with him. "I know you don't believe in incantations, but I have actually experienced it. Even if you don't believe in it, what can you lose by trying?"

"Oh, all right." Buldeyev gave in. "I'm not only ready to turn to the tax man for relief, I'd even send a telegram to the devil himself! Ouch! I can't stand it another minute! Tell me, where did you say the assessor lives now? Where do I write to him?"

The general sat down at his desk and took up his pen.

"In Saratov even every dog knows him," the steward began. "Be good enough to write, Your Excellency, to the city of Saratov . . . needless to say . . . to his Honor, Mister Yakov Vasilich . . . Vasilich . . ."

"Well? . . ."

"Vasilich . . . Yakov Vasilich . . . his last name. . . . Darn it! I forgot his last name! . . . Vasilich . . . Darn it! What *is* his last name? On my way here I remembered it perfectly! . . . Just a moment, please . . ."

The steward raised his eyes to the ceiling and moved his lips. Buldeyev and his wife waited impatiently.

"Come on, think faster!" the general ordered.

"Just a minute . . . Vasilich . . . Yakov Vasilich . . . I forgot! And it's such a common name . . . sort of horsy—it has something to do with horses . . . *Mare*vich? *Colt*orovsky? No, not *Colt*orovsky. Wait— maybe *Colt*sov? No, that's not right! I remember so clearly that his last name is horsy, but exactly what it is just slipped my mind . . ."

"*Colt*obyatnikov?"

"Not in the least! Wait . . . *Mare*nofsky? . . . *Mare*-novenko? No, not any of these either."

"Then how do you expect me to write to him? Think harder!"

"Yes, Your Excellency! . . . *Horse*kin . . . *Mare*-kin . . . *Wheel*kovoy . . ."

"*Wheeler*kov?" the general's wife asked.

"Not at all! Maybe *Trace*kin? No, that's not it. I simply forgot!"

"Then why the devil do you come here with advice if you forgot?" the general fumed. "Get out of here! Out!"

The steward left reluctantly, and the general pressed his hand tight against his cheek and began to pace from room to room in great agony.

"Father in Heaven!" he moaned. "I can't stand it!" he wailed. "It'll be the end of me!"

The steward stood in the garden, his eyes raised to the sky, and continued trying to remember the fateful name:

"*Colt*obchikov . . . *Colt*ovsky . . . *Colt*ushenko . . . No, none of these."

After a while he was called back by his master:

"Well, do you remember now?" the general asked.

"Not yet, Your Excellency."

"Maybe it is *Steed*nyavsky? . . . *Horse*dnikov? . . . No?"

And everyone in the household vied with one another in inventing horsy surnames. They went through horses of all ages, sexes, and breeds, not forgetting manes, hoofs, and harness. In the house, the garden, the servants' quarters, and in the kitchen, they paced from corner to corner and, scratching their heads, searched for the right name.

The steward was recalled again and again by his master.

"*Herd*unov?" they asked him. "*Hoof*in? *Colt*ovorsky?"

"Not at all," the steward answered, and, constantly raising his eyes, continued thinking out loud: "*Steed*orenko, *Steed*enko, *Foal*obin, *Hoof*oleev."

"Papa," the children called from the nursery, "*Troik*in? *Bridle*vikin?"

The whole manor was now worked up over the matter. And after the impatient, anguished general promised five rubles to the one who thought of the assessor's last name, a whole crowd began to follow the steward about the place:

"*Bay*lov?" they asked, "*Trotter*ovich? *Horse*ditsky?"

It was beginning to get dark, but no one had yet found the name. Finally everybody retired for the night, and no telegram was sent.

The major-general couldn't sleep a wink and kept pacing and moaning. At about three in the morning he went ouside and knocked at the steward's window:

"Could it be *Gelding*opolsky?" he asked tearfully.

"No, not *Gelding*opolsky, Your Excellency," the steward replied and sighed guiltily.

"Maybe it isn't a horsy name at all, but some other kind."

"I swear, Your Excellency, it's a horsy one. This I remember perfectly well."

"What a forgetful fellow you are then, I must say! This name is more precious to me now than anything else in the world. I'm worn out with the pain!"

In the morning the general called in the doctor again.

Let him pull it out! he had decided. I have no strength left to suffer.

The doctor came and pulled out the aching tooth. The pain subsided at once, and the general calmed down. His task accomplished, the doctor pocketed his fee, returned to his carriage, and drove away. Outside the gate, in the field, he met the steward. He was standing on the side of the road looking down at his feet with great concentration, obviously deep in thought. Judging from the wrinkles furrowing his brow and from the expression in his eyes, he was straining his brain and his thoughts were tormenting ones:

"*Dunsov . . . Saddlerovich . . . Harnessensky . . .*"

"Ivan Evseich," the doctor addressed him, "Can I, my dear fellow, purchase from you about forty bushels of oats? Our peasants sell oats, but theirs are very poor."

The steward stared stupidly at the doctor, smiled in a wild way, and, not uttering a word in reply, clapped his hands and dashed off toward the manor house as though pursued by a mad dog.

"I remember it now, Your Excellency!" he cried in a voice transformed with happiness, as he flew into the general's study. "I remember it now. May the Lord bless the doctor with the best of health! *OATSOV! Oats*ov is the surname of the assessor! *Oats*ov, Your Excellency! Send the telegram to *Oats*ov!"

"You're through!" the general shouted at the steward, thumbing his nose at him, "I no longer need your horsy name now! You're fired!"

ANTON CHEKHOV was born in 1860 in the Russian town of Taganrog, on the Sea of Azov. He was the son of a grocer, and had to work for many hours daily in the store. When his father's business failed, the family moved to Moscow, and they left Anton at home in Taganrog to finish school. During this time he had to support himself by tutoring his classmates. When he graduated he went to Moscow, where he entered medical school. But Chekhov still was forced to support himself and his family and began to write short pieces for magazines and newspapers.

By the time he became a physician, in 1884, he was also beginning to have some success as an author. Shortly thereafter, he chose writing as his life's work, although he continued to use his medical talents to help the poor. Weakened by want, a heavy load of literary work, and clinical duties, he contracted tuberculosis while he was still a young man. At the age of forty-four, this master of the short story, major playwright, and humanitarian died of this disease. Chekhov's works are still widely translated, published, and produced in the theater and in films.

MIRIAM MORTON was born in Russia and has a native knowledge of Russian literature. She has been called a "superb" translator by the *Saturday Review*, and critics in other publications have judged her translations "excellent," "remarkable," and "masterly." *Fierce and Gentle Warriors*, her book of stories by Mikhail Sholokhov, the Nobel Prize winner, was acclaimed by the *New York Review of Books* as "beautifully translated." She is also the anthologist of *A Harvest of Russian Children's Literature*.

Mrs. Morton has lived in this country since her youth. She is at present a resident of Los Angeles.

A NOTE ABOUT THIS BOOK

The text of this book is set in the linotype version of Janson, a type face which dates from about 1700. It is thought to be of Dutch origin, although some sizes were perhaps cut in Germany. The typography, layout and binding were designed by Earl Tidwell.